TRAINING MANUAL

By Simcha Whitehill

SCHOLASTIC INC.

ISBN 978-1-338-27965-8

10 9 8 7 6 5 4 3 2 1 18 19 20 21 22

Printed in China 68

First printing 2018

INTRODUCTION

Are you adventurous?
Are you brave?
Are you the kind of person who sets a goal and won't give up till you've achieved it?
Are you a good friend?

If you answered "YES!" to all of the above, then it sounds like you have what it takes to be an awesome Pokémon Trainer!

This book is your guide to becoming the best Trainer you can be. It's got everything you need to know about catching, raising, battling, and evolving Pokémon.

WHAT IS A POKÉMON TRAINER?

A Pokémon Trainer is a person who practices and battles with their Pokémon pals. Through training, a strong bond develops that makes both the Pokémon and the person stronger.

A Pokémon Trainer is not the boss of any Pokémon she catches. A Trainer and a Pokémon must learn about each other to develop the deep understanding and trust that will make them a team. They are partners and, above all, friends.

GETTING STARTED

When you turn double digits on your tenth birthday, you can claim your first partner Pokémon. Your local professor will present you with one of three types of Pokémon: a Water-type, a Fire-type, or a Grass-type.

The species of first partner Pokémon you get to choose from all depends on the region you're from. Once you have your first partner, you can begin your journey to become a Pokémon Trainer!

FIRST PARTNER

Here are some of the known regions of the Pokémon world. These are the first partner Pokémon from each region:

KANTO
Squirtle, Bulbasaur, Charmander

JOHTO
Cyndaquil, Totodile, Chikorita

HOENN
Treecko, Torchic, Mudkip

POKEMON

SINNOH
Turtwig, Piplup, Chimchar
UNOVA
Snivy, Tepig, Oshawott
KALOS
Chespin, Fennekin, Froakie
ALOLA
Popplio, Rowlet, Litten

ON THE ROAD

Becoming an amazing Pokémon Trainer takes practice and experience. The best way to learn about Pokémon is to travel around and meet them. You never know whom you'll encounter—and battle!

So far, there are seven known regions a Pokémon Trainer can explore:

KANTO

Many Trainers begin their quest in this colorful region.

JOHTO

This region is the perfect hiking spot for nature-loving Trainers.

HOENN

Ready to heat up your battle style? Check out this region's amazing volcanos!

UNOVA

If you can't decide whether you prefer city life or natural wonder, then Unova is the place for you. It's got it all!

SINNOH

This lovely region is known for its beautiful lakes and mountains.

KALOS

This region is shaped like a star—probably because it's a stellar place to visit!

ALOLA

If you need to get away from it all, you've come to the right place. The gorgeous islands of Alola are the perfect vacation spot.

HOW TO CATCH 'EM ALL

#1) BATTLING

Challenge the Pokémon to a battle. If you win, you earn the chance to catch it.

#2) BEFRIENDING

Another option is to simply befriend a Pokémon. If you can build the bonds of friendship through a shared cause or a rescue mission, you can save the day and make a new Pokémon pal!

NOTE: Not every Pokémon you help will want you to become their Trainer. Part of being a good Trainer is helping people, Pokémon, and the planet. Doing the right thing is its own reward—and from time to time, it might include the chance to catch a Pokémon.

#3) TRADING

Along your journey, you just might meet a Trainer and Pokémon who want to trade with you. For example, as Ash got to know his Pokémon pal Aipom, he realized that it loved the spotlight and competing in Pokémon Contests. His friend Dawn, a Pokémon Coordinator, found that her Pokémon buddy Buizel loved to battle and wasn't as into competing in Pokémon Contests. (For more on Pokémon Coordinators and Contests, turn to pages thirty-three and forty-three.) Ash and Dawn decided to trade Aipom and Buizel. So, should the right match arise, you can trade Pokémon.

NOTE: It will be hard to say so long to a friend.

TIP: If you are traveling through Unova and would like to trade Pokémon, visit Professor Juniper and ask to borrow her Pokémon Trading Device. It has an incredible advancement that will exchange your Pokémon and help them evolve all at once.

#4) FISHING

Water-type Pokémon can be found in lakes, oceans, rivers, and streams. If you have your fishing pole handy, you might be able to catch a new pal. Ash's friend Cilan, who is a fantastic fisherman, once caught a prickly Stunfisk in a lake outside Nimbasa City.

#5) HATCHING EGGS

Most Pokémon hatch from Eggs. When an Egg starts to glow, the Pokémon is ready to come out.

While Pokémon come in a wide variety of sizes and shapes, Pokémon Eggs tend to look about the same. Some Eggs have colorful markings on the outside that give hints about the type of Pokémon inside.

Eggs can be found in the wild or even handed out as prizes. But no matter how you get one, you must take good care of it. The outside of an Egg may be hard, but inside is a little living thing that won't appreciate a bumpy ride. It's a good idea to get a special carrier for it.

BETTER LUCK NEXT TIME

If your Poké Ball bounces back or the Pokémon you're trying to catch pops back out, there could be a couple of things going on. Either you haven't quite won it over yet, or the Pokémon might already have a Trainer.

SIX IS THE MAGIC NUMBER

A Pokémon Trainer can only travel with six Pokémon pals at a time. To catch additional Pokémon, a Trainer must find a fun spot for a Pokémon buddy to live and play. You could transfer it to a Pokémon Professor at their lab or find it the perfect Pokémon habitat.

From time to time, Trainers can recall Pokémon they've transferred and bring them back on their journey. Depending on where you are, it can be as simple as a call to the local Pokémon Center.

THE POKÉ BALL

Poké Balls are small, round capsules that Trainers use to carry their Pokémon around in. Each Pokémon has its own Poké Ball. No matter the Pokémon's size, it finds its Poké Ball to be a very cozy, restful home.

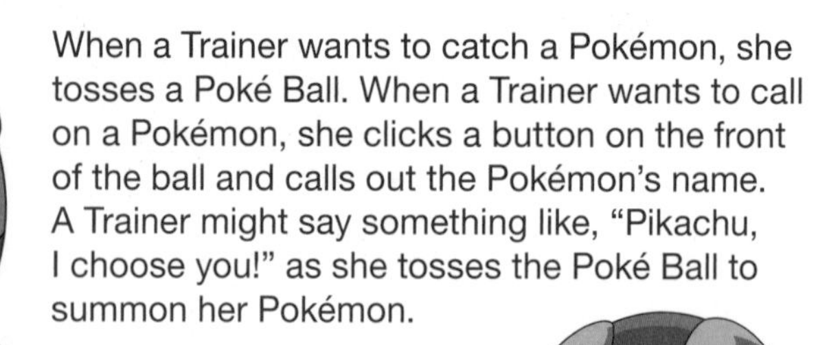

When a Trainer wants to catch a Pokémon, she tosses a Poké Ball. When a Trainer wants to call on a Pokémon, she clicks a button on the front of the ball and calls out the Pokémon's name. A Trainer might say something like, "Pikachu, I choose you!" as she tosses the Poké Ball to summon her Pokémon.

Speaking of Pikachu, Ash Ketchum's best friend is famous for traveling outside of its Poké Ball. The little yellow Electric-type Pokémon is always by Ash's side or hitching a ride on his shoulders. Some Pokémon prefer to travel right next to their Trainers.

TYPES OF POKÉ BALLS

There are many kinds of Poké Balls. The basic Poké Ball is half-red and half-white, with black details and a button at the center. While you can always use the standard Poké Ball, different types of Poké Balls can give Trainers special advantages.

POKÉ BALL: The gold standard Poké Ball, this common, basic model is used for catching and carrying Pokémon.

TIMER BALL: Skip this ball if your battle is short and sweet. The longer the battle, the better this Poké Ball works.

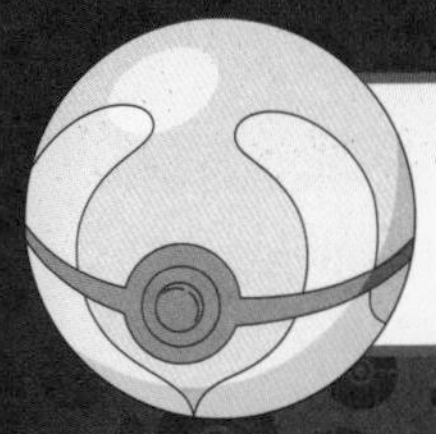

HEAL BALL: While there is no substitute for a visit to Nurse Joy, this Poké Ball is excellent at healing a Pokémon after battle.

GREAT BALL: More effective than the basic Poké Ball, the Great Ball will increase your chances of catching a Pokémon.

NET BALL: Have you set your sights on catching a Bug-type or Water-type Pokémon? Try using this Poké Ball for an added advantage.

QUICK BALL: Don't dillydally during battle if you're holding a Quick Ball. The sooner you throw it, the more effective it will be.

SAFARI BALL: If you're not in the Safari Zone, you can't use this Poké Ball.

REPEAT BALL: The Repeat Ball is highly effective in helping a Trainer catch a Pokémon species he or she has caught before.

ULTRA BALL: This advanced Poké Ball offers an even greater rate of success than the Great Ball.

DIVE BALL: If you're looking to catch a Pokémon underwater, first change into a swimsuit. Then try using an extremely effective Dive Ball.

DUSK BALL: Whether you're under a night sky or inside a dark cave, the Dusk Ball is awesome at catching Pokémon in low light.

NEST BALL: For weaker Pokémon, the Nest Ball is the perfect pick.

LUXURY BALL: This Poké Ball can help you make a quick connection with your new Pokémon buddy.

PREMIER BALL: Same basic Poké Ball, different look.

MASTER BALL: This Poké Ball lives up to its name—it is the Master. The most powerful Poké Ball out there, it can help you capture any Pokémon you'd like—even a Legendary Pokémon!

TRAINING YOUR POKÉMON

The core of becoming a good Pokémon Trainer is—you guessed it—training. It requires a lot of time, practice, care, and consideration to become a Pokémon Trainer. You must dedicate your life to learning about and bringing out the best in each and every Pokémon you catch. The goal is for you and your Pokémon to form an unstoppable team and an unbreakable friendship.

The best way to create that camaraderie with a Pokémon pal is to get out there and battle! Practice moves, challenge other Trainers, and when you feel ready, enter Pokémon competitions and other events that will let you and your Pokémon buddies shine!

POKÉMON BATTLES

ONE-ON-ONE BATTLES

The most common kind of battle is when one Trainer and her Pokémon pal challenge another Trainer and her Pokémon pal. Trainers can also choose to use multiple Pokémon in their match and have two-on-two, three-on-three, four-on-four, or five-on-five battles.

FULL BATTLE

A Full Battle is also known as a six-on-six battle. This type of battle is extremely challenging because both Trainers can call on all six Pokémon they have on hand. However, only one Pokémon from each Trainer's team can be on the battlefield at a time. A winner is declared when all six Pokémon on one Trainer's team are left unable to battle.

DOUBLE BATTLE

In this kind of battle, each Trainer has two Pokémon face two of her opponent's Pokémon at the same time. The Pokémon must work together as a team. Even if one Pokémon on a team faints, the Trainer can still win the match with the remaining Pokémon. To qualify for the Hoenn League Championships, a Trainer must win three Double Battles in a row.

TAG BATTLE

A Tag Battle is a match between two teams, with two Pokémon Trainers on each team. Each Trainer can only choose one Pokémon. The battle is finished when both Pokémon on one team are unable to continue.

This kind of match requires both people and Pokémon to work together to seal the win! In Sinnoh, Hearthome City hosts a cool Tag Battle Tournament. Unfortunately, Trainers don't get to pick their tag teammate. Once Ash had to battle with his rival, the cold-hearted and calculating Paul. However, that battle ended with Ash's Pokémon pal Chimchar joining Ash on his journey.

CONTEST BATTLE

This type of battle is specific to Pokémon Contests. Since the goal of Pokémon Coordinators is to display their Pokémon pal's elegance, the battles are merely ways for them to show off their beauty and finesse. Contest Battles are timed, and Pokémon only have five minutes to show off their skills. Pokémon can use single, double, or triple combination Attacks to lower their opponent's score. These battles are considered to be more like performances, and the Pokémon Coordinator with the higher score wins the match.

TEAM BATTLE

A team battle has Pokémon Trainers working in groups of three, five, or even seven people. As partners in battle, they come up with clever combinations and fun formations for their Pokémon. It really challenges Pokémon Trainers and Pokémon to work together and get creative! What combinations would you dream of doing, if you could battle with two of your best friends and their Pokémon? The sky is the limit!

At Professor Sycamore's summer camp in Kalos, the final activity is a team battle where bunks unite and battle one another for a special place in the hall of fame.

SKY BATTLES

Up, up, up in the air is precisely where sky battles take place. Trainers must choose Flying-type Pokémon for this type of battle. But they don't strain their necks staring up at the sky. They can get in on the action by wearing wing suits that can catch the breeze.

Because of their specialized outfits, sky battles have to take place in an area with an updraft. It also helps if you're tall—that way, you'll have a long wingspan. A popular spot for sky battles is Kalos Canyon.

RECALLING POKÉMON DURING A BATTLE

During a battle, you might want to swap in a different Pokémon because you see a strategic advantage for another one of your Pokémon pals. If the rules of the battle permit, you can bring in another Pokémon.

This kind of exchange is a common way for Pokémon to be returned to their Poké Balls during battle. But it's not the only reason. If your Pokémon looks scared, tired, overwhelmed, or doesn't want to battle, you'll want to return them to their Poké Ball immediately. As a Trainer, you might work hard to win, but you'll lose out if you mistreat your Pokémon friends.

POKÉMON CENTERS

Wherever there is a Pokémon in need, there is a Pokémon Center nearby! Pokémon Centers are special hubs run by identical family members all named Nurse Joy. These dedicated nurses and their Pokémon aides tend to every Pokémon who comes to see them. Their mission is to help Pokémon rest and recover, whether they're drained, ill, or just plain tired. A top-notch Trainer will take their Pokémon to the Pokémon Center for regular checkups and some R&R, especially after a battle.

At many Pokémon Centers, there are places for Trainers to enjoy some free time. Trainers can call home, friends, or even a Pokémon Professor with video chat. They can transfer a Poké Ball through the call. There's always a place to sit down and eat a good meal. Since so many Trainers pass through, Pokémon Centers are also a great place to make friends and even spark a battle challenge!

Pokémon Centers, unlike Nurse Joys, do not look alike. You can tell you're in the right place because the building will have at least one Poké Ball decoration and/or be marked by the letter "P."

In Slateport City, in the Hoenn region, it is Nurse Joy who gives local Trainers their pick of first partner Pokémon: Torchic, Mudkip, or Treecko.

In Kalos, Pokémon Centers also play Pokévision videos made by Pokémon performers.

Nurse Joy has the best help—Pokémon pals! Depending on the region and the Pokémon Center, you'll find a caring Chansey, Blissey, Audino, Wigglytuff, or Comfey by her side.

POKÉMON TYPES

There are currently eighteen known types of Pokémon: Bug, Dark, Dragon, Electric, Fairy, Fighting, Fire, Flying, Ghost, Grass, Ground, Ice, Normal, Poison, Psychic, Rock, Steel, and Water. In battle, each type has certain strengths and weaknesses. Smart Trainers will learn their advantages and disadvantages by heart.

BUG

DARK

DRAGON

ELECTRIC

FAIRY

FIGHTING

FIRE

FLYING

GHOST

GRASS

GROUND

ICE

NORMAL

POISON

PSYCHIC

ROCK

STEEL

WATER

A SECOND OPINION

Some Trainers don't rely on type when choosing which Pokémon to use in battle. For example, Ash Ketchum is known for picking Pokémon that don't have a type advantage and then creating a clever battle strategy to seal a win. Some Trainers believe that the true edge a Trainer and Pokémon need is the deep bond of friendship that creates unstoppable teamwork.

POKEMON TRAINERS

Not every Trainer decides to focus on battling and Pokémon competitions. There are many different fields that Trainers can focus their efforts on:

A **POKÉMON BREEDER** is all about raising healthy, happy Pokémon. They are excellent, attentive Pokémon caretakers. First and foremost, a Pokémon Breeder is focused on a Pokémon's fitness, diet, and well-being. Ash's travel buddy Brock is a Pokémon Breeder who is also an awesome chef.

A **POKÉMON COORDINATOR** competes in Pokémon contests to showcase their Pokémon's talent, beauty, and their personal style. Coordinators are rewarded with Ribbons for their wins, and all hope to be honored as Top Coordinator. Ash's friend Dawn is a Pokémon Coordinator.

A **POKÉMON PERFORMER** is a graceful choreographer who dances on the stage in sync with their Pokémon at Pokémon Showcases. They are also extremely stylish and create the most fashionable outfits for their competitions. Pokémon performers compete for Princess Keys, the occasional tiara, and regional titles like Kalos Queen.

At heart, Pokémon performers love entertaining an audience—in person and on screen.

They also enjoy making Pokévision videos. Played at Pokémon Centers throughout Kalos, these Pokévision shorts really showcase performers' skills and bring them tons of fans.

Pokémon performers are also incredible bakers who make delicious Poké Puffs. Serena, Ash's childhood friend who later joins him on his journey, is a famous Pokémon performer.

A **POKÉMON GROOMER** is a gifted person who can style a Pokémon's hair into the latest fashion. A Pokémon groomer can also tell, through its hair, if the Pokémon is feeling well and eating well. They're focused on a Pokémon's nutrition because it truly affects its hair quality. For example, a groomer might recommend a special kind of Berry for when a Pokémon's not feeling well.

A Pokémon groomer and her subject bond through pampering. The only thing more fabulous than the finished look is their friendship. In Kalos, there is a superstar Pokémon groomer named Sherman, who is especially talented at caring for Furfrou.

A **POKÉMON CONNOISSEUR** is a person specially trained to judge the compatibility of a Pokémon and its Trainer. They can sense the character of both people and Pokémon and can instantly assess their strengths, weaknesses, and compatibility. This path requires a lot of study, and Pokémon Connoisseurs must attend a special school to learn about all types of Pokémon. Ash's pal Cilan is a Pokémon Connoisseur.

A **POKÉMON BARD** is a sensitive soul who has a way with words and can carry a tune. A Pokémon bard speaks in poems and shares both wisdom and her sense of calm. Ash met the Pokémon bard Nando while traveling through Sinnoh.

A **POKÉMON WATCHER** is someone who patiently observes Pokémon. Knowledgeable Pokémon watchers can tell a Pokémon's health and strength just by looking at it. Tracey Sketchit, a friend Ash made in the Orange Islands, is a Pokémon watcher.

A **GYM LEADER** is always ready for a battle challenge! Gym Leaders are highly successful Pokémon Trainers who focus on a particular Pokémon type. They often develop their gym's atmosphere to favor their Pokémon pals. For example, in Sinnoh, the Icirrus Gym Leader Brycen is an Ice-type expert, and his slippery battlefield is frozen over.

Win a match against a Gym Leader, and you'll be rewarded with a unique badge that represents her gym. Trainers who want to compete in a Pokémon League Championship must collect eight badges in a single region.

A **POKÉMON SCIENTIST** or **RESEARCHER** studies Pokémon, fossils, data, and any information they can gather from the lab and the field. Their life's goal is to gain insight on Pokémon behavior, origins, habitats, health, and more. Often, Pokémon scientists become Pokémon Professors and run important labs, like Professor Oak does.

POKÉMON PROFESSORS

Pokémon Professors are scientists who study Pokémon in their labs and the field. In addition to their research, many are responsible for handing out first partner Pokémon, a Pokédex, and Poké Balls to new Trainers.

As Trainers begin their journeys, Pokémon Professors are great sources of information. They're always just a phone call away, able to answer any questions, offer advice, and even care for your Pokémon at their labs. Professors know a lot about Pokémon and are happy to help. After all, they're obsessed with Pokémon, too!

MEET THE PROFESSORS

Here are the professors you'll meet on your journey:

KANTO: PROFESSOR OAK
From his lab in Pallet Town, Professor Samuel Oak studies Pokémon behavior. He is considered one of the most important Pokémon scientists.

ORANGE ISLANDS: PROFESSOR IVY
Since her home is a collection of islands, Professor Felina Ivy is always sailing around to gather information. The focus of her studies is regional differences in various Pokémon's appearance.

JOHTO: PROFESSOR ELM

Professor Elm used to be one of Professor Oak's top students. Although they might not always see eye-to-eye, they respect each other and have interesting debates. Professor Elm runs a large lab in New Bark Town.

HOENN: PROFESSOR BIRCH

Professor Birch hands out first partner Pokémon Treecko, Torchic, and Mudkip to new Trainers in Hoenn. His lab is located in Littleroot Town, but you are more likely to find him enjoying the great outdoors with his Pokémon pal Poochyena. Fascinated by the habits of wild Pokémon, this professor isn't afraid to climb, hike, or do whatever it takes to observe them.

SINNOH: PROFESSOR ROWAN
Based in Sandgem Town, Professor Rowan is one of the smartest Pokémon Researchers. His studies center on the Pokémon Evolutionary processes—he believes Pokémon can be linked to each other through Evolution. Chimchar, Piplup, and Turtwig are the first partner Pokémon he hands out to new Trainers.

UNOVA: PROFESSOR JUNIPER
Fascinated by Pokémon origins, Professor Juniper has invented some groundbreaking technology. Her Pokémon Trading Device evolves and exchanges Pokémon between Trainers. She also created the Restoration Machine that harnesses Musharna's Dream Mist to bring Pokémon back to life from fossils. With advancements like that, it's no wonder that Professor Oak regards her as one of the most important Pokémon scientists working today.

KALOS: PROFESSOR SYCAMORE

The foremost expert in Mega Evolution, Professor Sycamore doesn't just study it in a lab, he can also use it to help his best buddy, Garchomp, Mega Evolve. He and Garchomp have been together since it was Gible, so they have a deep bond of friendship. The professor's lab in Lumiose City has a big habitat that many Pokémon call home. Professor Sycamore is also responsible for giving out Kalos's first partner Pokémon, Chespin, Fennekin, and Froakie, to Trainers in the region.

ALOLA: PROFESSOR KUKUI
This Pokémon scientist is a real outdoors kind of guy, but how could you not be in a region full of natural wonders like Alola?! Although Professor Kukui teaches at the Pokémon School, he prefers to conduct both his classes and his research in the field. He's an expert on Pokémon moves—and he is always on the move himself!

THE POKÉDEX

These handheld devices offer a wealth of knowledge on Pokémon. In fact, when you spot a Pokémon you've never seen before, you can identify it and get all the stats from your Pokédex. There is a screen to view all the details, but the voice of the Pokédex will also tell you everything you need to know.

Every Trainer has a Pokédex, but they are different in every region. In Alola, the Pokédex is especially animated because it is inhabited by a Pokémon known as Rotom. So it is called a Rotom Dex.

THE POKÉMON LEAGUE

This important worldwide organization ensures every Trainer not only gets a great start, but also has incredible experiences along the way. The Pokémon League is responsible for all the Gyms in every region and for the regional championships. It also plays an important role in raising the first partner Pokémon new Trainers receive.

Being a Gym Leader is hard work, but it's rewarding. Anyone interested in starting his or her own Gym must first put a request in to the Pokémon League. To ensure quality and fairness, Gyms must be certified

Ash's first Regional Championship: the Indigo League

by the League through a tough inspection process. But even after the Gym is approved, the Pokémon Inspection Agency (PIA) will make random visits to check on the Gym's operations. They have the power to shut down any Gym they feel isn't up to the Pokémon League's standards of cleanliness and safety.

After a Trainer earns eight badges in a region, they are invited to compete in the local championship, which is entirely run by the League. It decides the rules, oversees the opening ceremony and torch lighting, organizes the competition rounds, and hands out a prize to the winner. The League also trains judges and referees to run the tournaments and make sure everyone's following the rules.

GYM LEADERS AND GYM BADGES

There are Gyms in nearly every town and city. Each is run by a Gym Leader or two, and sometimes even three. Gyms are named after their city or town, like the Nacrene Gym in Nacrene City. Trainers looking to compete in the Pokémon League Championship challenge these Gym Leaders to a battle. However, some Gym Leaders might be out and about; some might ask you to complete a task before they'll battle you; and some might just not be ready the minute you arrive. But with a little patience, you should eventually be able to get that battle you've been hoping for!

Gym Leaders are formidable opponents because they have a lot of experience. Most are experts in a particular Pokémon type. They love Pokémon and enjoy battling. Often, their Gyms reflect their colorful personalities, their favorite Pokémon type, or even their location.

If a Trainer wins their match, a Gym Leader will award them a unique badge that represents her Gym.

Brock is one of the first Gym Leaders Ash met on his journey.

HERE'S A LIST OF KNOWN GYMS AND THEIR GYM LEADERS:

GYM	GYM LEADER	BADGE	SPECIALTY	REGION
Pewter City Gym	Brock	Boulder Badge	Rock-type	Kanto
Cerulean City Gym	Misty	Cascade Badge	Water-type	Kanto
Vermillion City Gym	Lt. Surge	Thunder Badge	Electric-type	Kanto
Saffron City Gym	Sabrina	Marsh Badge	Psychic-type	Kanto
Celadon City Gym	Erika	Rainbow Badge	Grass-type	Kanto
Fuchsia City Gym	Koga	Soul Badge	Poison-type	Kanto
Cinnabar City Gym	Blaine	Volcano Badge	Fire-type	Kanto
Viridian City Gym	Giovanni	Earth Badge	Ground-type	Kanto

Giovanni, the leader of the Viridian City Gym, is also the head of Team Rocket.

GYM	GYM LEADER	BADGE	SPECIALTY	REGION
Mikan City Gym	Cissy	Coral-Eye Badge		Orange Islands
Navel City Gym	Danny	Sea Ruby Badge		Orange Islands
Trovita City Gym	Rudy	Spike Shell Badge		Orange Islands
Goldenrod City Gym	Whitney	Plain Badge		Johto
Azalea City Gym	Bugsy	Hive Badge	Bug-type	Johto
Violet City Gym	Falkner	Zephyr Badge	Flying-type	Johto
Ecruteak City Gym	Morty	Fog Badge	Ghost-type	Johto
Cianwood City Gym	Chuck	Storm Badge	Fighting-type	Johto
Olivine City Gym	Jasmine	Mineral Badge	Steel-type	Johto
Mahogany City Gym	Pryce	Glacier Badge	Ice-type	Johto
Blackthorn City Gym	Clair	Rising Badge	Dragon-type	Johto

Whitney and her Pokémon, Miltank

GYM	GYM LEADER	BADGE	SPECIALTY	REGION
Rustboro City Gym	Roxanne	Stone Badge	Rock-type	Hoenn
Dewford City Gym	Brawly	Knuckle Badge	Fighting-type	Hoenn
Mauville City Gym	Wattson	Dynamo Badge	Electric-type	Hoenn
Lavaridge City Gym	Flannery	Heat Badge	Fire-type	Hoenn
Petalburg City Gym	Norman	Balance Badge	Normal-type	Hoenn
Fortree City Gym	Winona	Feather Badge	Flying-type	Hoenn
Mossdeep City Gym	Tate and Liza	Mind Badge	Psychic-type	Hoenn
Sootopolis City Gym	Juan	Rain Badge	Water-type	Hoenn

Norman, Gym Leader in Petalburg City

GYM	GYM LEADER	BADGE	SPECIALTY	REGION
Oreburgh City Gym	Roark	Coal Badge	Rock-type	Sinnoh
Eterna City Gym	Gardenia	Forest Badge	Grass-type	Sinnoh
Veilstone City Gym	Maylene	Coblle Badge	Fighting-type	Sinnoh
Pastoria City Gym	Crasher Wake	Fen Badge	Water-type	Sinnoh
Canalave City Gym	Byron	Mine Badge	Steel-type	Sinnoh
Hearthome City Gym	Fantina	Relic Badge	Ghost-type	Sinnoh
Snowpoint City Gym	Candice	Icicle Badge	Ice-type	Sinnoh
Sunyshore City Gym	Volkner	Beacon Badge	Electric-type	Sinnoh

Volkner, Gym Leader in Sunyshore City

GYM	GYM LEADER	BADGE	SPECIALTY	REGION
Striaton City Gym	Chili, Cress, Cilan	Trio Badge	Fire-type, Water-type, Grass-type	Unova
Nacrene City Gym	Leonora	Basic Badge	Normal-type	Unova
Castelia City Gym	Burgh	Insect Badge	Bug-type	Unova
Nimbasa City Gym	Elesa	Bolt Badge	Electric-type	Unova
Driftveil City Gym	Clay	Quake Badge	Ground-type	Unova
Mistralton City Gym	Skyla	Jet Badge	Flying-type	Unova
Icirrus City Gym	Brycen	Freeze Badge	Ice-type	Unova
Virbank City Gym	Roxie	Toxic Badge	Poison-type	Unova

Ash's traveling companion Cilan is one of the Gym Leaders in Striaton City.

Korrina, at the Shalour City Gym, is an expert in Mega Evolution.

GYM	GYM LEADER	BADGE	SPECIALTY	REGION
Santalune City Gym	Viola	Bug Badge	Bug-type	Kalos
Cyllage City Gym	Grant	Cliff Badge	Rock-type	Kalos
Shalour City Gym	Korrina	Rumble Badge	Fighting-type	Kalos
Coumarine City Gym	Ramos	Plant Badge	Grass-type	Kalos
Lumiouse City Gym	Clemont	Voltage Badge	Electric-type	Kalos
Laverre City Gym	Valerie	Fairy Badge	Fairy-type	Kalos
Anistar City Gym	Olympia	Psychic Badge	Psychic-type	Kalos
Snowbelle City Gym	Wulfric	Iceberg Badge	Ice-type	Kalos

BADGE CASE

For safety, Trainers store the Gym Badges they've earned in a small box called a badge case. They typically have eight slots to hold all the badges from a single region.

THE ISLAND CHALLENGE

In the Alola region, Trainers are put to the test in a different way. They don't travel for challenges at Gyms. Instead, they participate in an awesome experience called the Island Challenge. The aim is to prove they have what it takes for the Grand Trial. They must prove themselves to the Island Kahuna.

Every island of Alola has an Island Kahuna who decides and presides over these events. They give both the go-ahead and the task, and they're also the only ones who can decide if the Trainer has succeeded in their mission.

An Island Challenge is meant to strengthen a Trainer's skills, and also to show an appreciation for the natural beauty in perfect balance in Alola. For example, when Melemele Island's Kahuna, Hala, gave Ash the Island Challenge, Ash had to figure out how to keep Alolan Rattata and Alolan Raticate from overrunning the town.

After a Trainer proves herself in the Island Challenge, she earns the opportunity to battle the Island Kahuna in a Grand Trial. If the Trainer wins, the Island Kahuna presents her with a Z-Crystal (more on Z-Crystals on page ninety-four).

SPECIAL SPOTS FOR TRAINERS

THE BATTLE CHATEAU

Just outside of Cyllage City in the Kalos region, Duke Turner runs a training center fit for royalty! In fact, with each win at the Battle Chateau, Trainers can earn regal titles, from beginner Barons to celebrated Grand Dukes and Duchesses.

All the Trainers who battle at the Chateau are considered knights and are expected to maintain a strict code of honor.

BATTLE CLUBS

In Unova, when a Trainer and their Pokémon pals want to prepare for an important match, they head to the local Battle Club. The clubs are led by identical cousins all named Don George. Don George will get you in shape for any battle challenge.

The Battle Clubs have exercise regimens to strengthen you and your Pokémon's speed, power, and teamwork.

Often, Trainers will post on the Club's electronic bulletin board when they're looking for another Trainer to have a practice battle with.

Ash with Don George

PROFESSOR ROWAN'S POKÉMON SUMMER ACADEMY

Located on Mt. Coronet, Professor Rowan's Pokémon Summer Academy is designed to get campers out of their comfort zone and put them to the test. There are many challenges, including being paired with one of the academy's Pokémon as a battle partner, a visit to the Summit Ruins (where many Ghost-type Pokémon hang out), and a Pokémon Triathlon. Professor Rowan is a strict camp director, but those who pay attention can learn a lot from him.

PROFESSOR SYCAMORE'S SUMMER CAMP

Every summer, a group of lucky Trainers in the Kalos region attend an awesome summer camp run by Professor Sycamore. Located in Coastal Kalos, the camp boasts beautiful views of both the beach and mountains. Each bunk becomes a team that competes in various competitions. Campers and their Pokémon pals train hard and play hard!

THE POKÉMON SCHOOL

In the Alola Region, right on the shores of Melemele Island, there is an incredible academy called the Pokémon School. Students lucky enough to attend can learn so much from their principal, Samson Oak, a Pokémon variant expert, and their teacher, Professor Kukui.

COOL TECH

XTRANSCEIVER

No matter where you are or where the person you want to call is, you can reach anyone on the Xtransceiver. It has unstoppable reception and clarity. Experienced Trainers know the "X" in the name stands for "cross," and this device is actually pronounced "cross-transceiver."

POKÉTCH

Invented in Jubilife City, the Pokétch might look like an ordinary watch, but it's quite the tech accessory. Sure, it keeps time, but it can also store cool applications like Coin Toss.

POKÉNAV

This technologically advanced device helps a Trainer know where to go as they make their way on their journey. The PokéNav keeps them heading in the right direction, and it also fits neatly inside their pockets.

POKÉGEAR

This amazing gadget can help Trainers with a range of tasks, including locating the closest Pokémon Center. It has a built-in phone and map.

TRAINERS, BEWARE!

Pokémon hunters, poachers, and thieves will go to great lengths to steal Pokémon and cause trouble. Keep an eye out for these Most Wanted bad guys.

HUNTER J:
Frequently in Sinnoh. Often swoops in on Salamence.

THE POKÉMON POACHER BROTHERS:
Braggo, Blurt, and Chico: Last seen in Johto. They travel by sneaky submarine.

RICO: Last seen in Hoenn. Has a penchant for Poison-type Pokémon.

RIZZO: Last seen in Unova, Travels with a pair of Jellicent.

TEAM ROCKET: Jessie, James, and Meowth: Have traveled through Kanto, Johto, Hoenn, Sinnoh, Unova, Kalos, and Alola. Known for setting traps, riding in a variety of mechs, and wearing silly disguises.

TEAM SKULL: Group of misfits found in Alola. Can be identified by black-and-white clothing with skull logo.

ABANDONED POKÉMON

Nasty Trainers have been known to abandon their Pokémon pals if the Trainer loses a battle, thinks her Pokémon are too weak, doesn't like them, or simply doesn't want them anymore. To the thoughtless Trainer, it might seem like this Pokémon is holding them back from greatness. But in fact, a Trainer who abandons their Pokémon is the one who's weak. This kind of heartless Trainer isn't willing to learn or grow to be the partner their Pokémon friend needs.

You see, it takes two to be a true team. Instead of seeing training Pokémon as a passion, a challenge, and a pathway to a beautiful friendship, some Trainers see it as a way to win trophies. But what kind of person abandons a true friend?

Fortunately, a Pokémon who is abandoned can find a more caring Trainer and friend. But the pain of being abandoned is a weight no Pokémon should ever have to experience after they put their trust in a Trainer.

LEGENDARY AND MYTHICAL POKÉMON

In every region, there are Pokémon who are so strong, very few Trainers can catch them, and they are only seen when they want to be. These precious and powerful Pokémon are called Mythical and Legendary Pokémon.

Mythical Pokémon Marshadow

If there is trouble somewhere in the universe, these powerful Pokémon might step in to help people and their fellow Pokémon to restore order. Should you ever get the chance to see one of these giants, consider yourself very lucky.

Mythical Pokémon Mageama

LEGENDARY POKEMON

KANTO

ARTICUNO
FREEZE POKÉMON

MOLTRES
FLAME POKÉMON

ZAPDOS
ELECTRIC POKÉMON

MEWTWO
GENETIC POKÉMON

JOHTO

ENTEI
VOLCANO POKÉMON

HO-OH
RAINBOW POKÉMON

LUGIA
DIVING POKÉMON

RAIKOU
THUNDER POKÉMON

SUICUNE
AURORA POKÉMON

HOENN

KYOGRE
SEA BASIN POKÉMON

GROUDON
CONTINENT POKÉMON

LATIOS
EON POKÉMON

LATIAS
EON POKÉMON

RAYQUAZA
SKY HIGH POKÉMON

REGIROCK
ROCK PEAK POKÉMON

REGICE
ICEBERG POKÉMON

REGISTEEL
IRON POKÉMON

AZELF
WILLPOWER POKÉMON

UXIE
KNOWLEDGE POKÉMON

MESPRIT
EMOTION POKÉMON

CRESSELIA
LUNAR POKÉMON

PALKIA
SPATIAL POKÉMON

DIALGA
TEMPORAL POKÉMON

GIRATINA
RENEGADE
POKÉMON

HEATRAN
LAVA DOME POKÉMON

REGIGIGAS
COLOSSAL
POKÉMON

UNOVA

RESHIRAM
VAST WHITE POKÉMON

ZEKROM
DEEP BLACK POKÉMON

COBALION
IRON WILL POKÉMON

VIRIZION
GRASSLAND POKÉMON

TERRAKION
CAVERN POKÉMON

KYUREM
BOUNDARY POKÉMON

LANDORUS
ABUNDANCE POKÉMON

THUNDURUS
BOLT STRIKE POKÉMON

TORNADUS
CYCLONE POKÉMON

KALOS

XERNEAS
LIFE POKÉMON

YVELTAL
DESTRUCTION POKÉMON

ZYGARDE
ORDER POKÉMON

ALOLA

COSMOEM
PROTOSTAR POKÉMON

COSMOG
NEBULA POKÉMON

LUNALA
MOONE POKÉMON

NECROZMA
PRISM POKÉMON

SILVALLY
SYNTHETIC POKÉMON

SOLGALEO
SUNNE POKÉMON

TYPE: NULL
SYNTHETIC POKÉMON

ZYGARDE
ORDER POKÉMON

ISLAND GUARDIANS

Each of the four Islands in Alola has an Island Guardian. Called the Land Spirit Pokémon, these Legendary Pokémon are powerful beings who protect their homelands. Tapu Koko, the Island Guardian of Melemele Island, has also taken to looking after Ash Ketchum.

TOTEM POKÉMON

Totem Pokémon are so big and powerful, they're well known in Alola and easy to spot because of their size. "Totem" is put before their names out of respect. There are several in the region. Most aid the Island Guardian and help Trainers during their Island Challenge. They care abou their community and environment and use their strength fo good.

MYTHICAL POKÉMON

KANTO

MEW
NEW SPECIES POKÉMON

JOHTO

CELEBI
TIME TRAVEL POKÉMON

HOENN

JIRACHI
WISH POKÉMON

DEOXYS
DNA POKÉMON

SINNOH

MANAPHY
SEAFARING POKÉMON

DARKRAI
PITCH-BLACK POKÉMON

ARCEUS
ALPHA POKÉMON

PHIONE
SEA DRIFTER POKÉMON

SHAYMIN
GRATITUDE POKÉMON

UNOVA

GENESECT
PALEOZOIC POKÉMON

KELDEO
COLT POKÉMON

MELOETTA
MELODY POKÉMON

VICTINI
VICTORY POKÉMON

KALOS

DIANCIE
JEWEL POKÉMON

HOOPA
MISCHIEF POKÉMON

VOLCANION
STEAM POKÉMON

ALOLA

MAGEARNA
ARTIFICIAL POKÉMON

MARSHADOW
GLOOMDWELLER POKÉMON

POKÉMON EVOLUTION

When a Trainer receives her first partner Pokémon, it is in its first stage. However, just as people grow and change, so do Pokémon. Through experience, training, and willpower, some Pokémon can take on a new physical form in an instant. And many can even change form two or three times!

When a Pokémon begins to evolve, its body begins to glow. Then its shape shifts. When the light fades, the transformation is finished. The Pokémon will stand proudly in their new form. It will have a new name, new strengths, and even the ability to learn new moves.

Not all Pokémon can evolve, and not every Pokémon wants to. Once in a grown form, a Pokémon can never return to an old form. So some Pokémon make the decision not to evolve—like Ash's pal Pikachu. It is strong enough and experienced enough to become Raichu, but it's not interested in evolving.

EEVEE AND ITS EVOLUTIONS

There is one unique Pokémon whose Evolutions always reflect the place in which it evolved—Eevee. The Evolution Pokémon has a genetic makeup that is very sensitive to its surroundings. When it is ready to evolve, the radiation from surrounding stones, the local environment, the time of day, and even its Trainer's heart can effect its development. Eevee even shifts Type, as it can evolve into eight different forms: Vaporeon, Jolteon, Flareon, Umbreon, Glaceon, Leafeon, Espeon, and Sylveon.

MEGA EVOLUTION

Not all forms of Evolution are permanent. Mega Evolution—a powerful surge of energy in which a Pokémon transforms into a super strong and speedy version of itself—is only temporary. It's such an incredible transformation that it requires the perfect combination of situation and supplies.

Mega Evolution can only occur during battle, and only certain Pokémon can achieve this short-lived state. Also, a Trainer needs to wear a Key Stone. And finally, a Trainer must quest to find a unique Mega Stone that corresponds to his Pokémon partner.

But the true key to activate the Key Stone and Mega Stone is heart. In order to awaken a Pokémon's power, a Trainer and her Pokémon must share an unbreakable bond. Then, and only then, can a Pokémon Mega Evolve.

Here's an example of a Pokémon's Mega Evolution: Lucario, with the aid of Lucarionite, can become Mega Lucario.

During Mega Evolution, the Pokémon is temporarily referred to with the title "Mega."

Z-Moves are passed down by the Island Guardian of each of the four Alolan Islands. A Trainer must participate in the Island Challenge and earn a band of metal plates called a Z-Ring, which has a Z-Crystal in the center.

But that feat alone is not enough. Z-Moves can only be unleashed when a Trainer and Pokémon are battling for a bigger purpose, like helping a friend or protecting the environment. The bond between Pokémon and Trainer is then turned into pure power, and their might rises to do what's right. The Z-Move will infinitely increase their offense and will conquer any foe.

Each Z-Crystal corresponds to a Pokémon type. For example, since Pikachu is an Electric-type Pokémon, together Ash and Pikachu use Electrium Z.

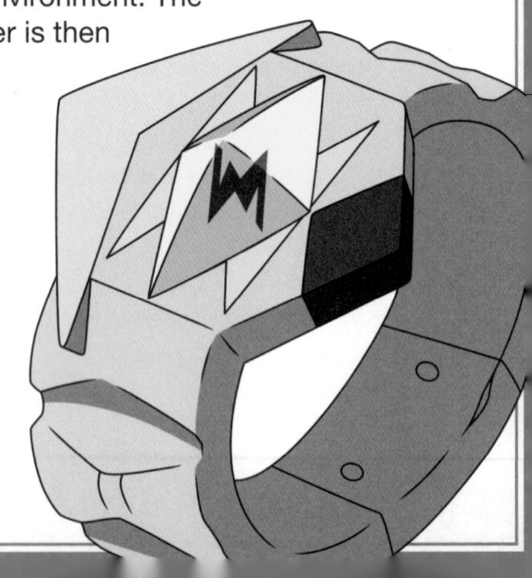

Thanks for reading this book, Trainer! You should have everything you need to complete your Pokémon quest. Good luck and keep on training!